THE
MENOMINEE

by Edward R. Ricciuti

Illustrated by Richard Smolinski

ROURKE PUBLICATIONS, INC.

VERO BEACH, FLORIDA 32964

CONTENTS

Library of Congress Cataloging-in-Publication Data

Ricciuti, Edward R.
    The Menominee / by Edward R. Ricciuti.
        p.   cm. — (Native American people)
    Includes index.
    Summary: Examines the history, traditional lifestyle, and current situation of the Woodland Indians known as the Menominee.
        ISBN 0-86625-603-2
        1. Menominee Indians—History—Juvenile literature.
    2. Menominee Indians—Social life and customs—Juvenile literature. [1. Menominee Indians. 2. Indians of North America—Wisconsin.] I. Title. II. Series.
    E99.M44R53 1997
    973'.004973—dc21   97-560
                                                                        CIP
                                                                        AC

Introduction

For many years, archaeologists—and other people who study early Native American cultures—believed that the first humans to live in the Americas arrived in Alaska from Siberia between 11,000 and 12,000 years ago. Stone spear points and other artifacts dating to that time were discovered in many parts of the Americas.

The first Americans probably arrived by way of a vast bridge of land between Siberia and Alaska. The land link emerged from the sea when Ice Age glaciers lowered the level of the world's oceans.

The first migration across the bridge was most likely an accident. It appears that bands of hunters from Asia followed herds of mammoths, giant bison, and other Ice Age game that roamed the 1,000-mile-wide bridge. Over a long time—perhaps thousands of years—some of the hunters arrived in Alaska.

Many scholars now suggest that the first Americans may have arrived in North America as early as 30,000 or even 50,000 years ago. Some of these early Americans may not have crossed the bridge to the New World. They may have arrived by boat, working their way down the west coasts of North America and South America.

In support of this theory, scientists who study language or genetics (the study of the inherited similarities and differences found in living things) believe that there may have been many migrations of peoples over the bridge to North America. There are about 200 different Native American languages, which vary greatly. In addition to speaking different languages, groups of Native Americans can look as physically different as, for example, Italians and Swedes. These facts lead some scientists to suspect that multiple migrations started in different parts of Asia. If this is true, then Native Americans descend not from one people, but from many.

After they arrived in Alaska, different groups of early Americans fanned out over North America and South America. They inhabited almost every corner of these two continents, from the shores of the Arctic Ocean in the north to Tierra del Fuego, at the southern tip of South America. Over this immense area, there were many different environments, which changed with the passage of time. The lifestyles of early Americans adapted to these environments and changed with them.

In what is now Mexico, some Native Americans built great cities and developed agriculture. Farming spread north. So did the concentration of people in large communities, which was the result of successful farming. In other regions of the Americas, agriculture was not as important. Wild animals and plants were the main sources of food for native hunters and gatherers, such as the Native Americans who established the Woodland culture. These people inhabited forests from the edges of the prairies in the Midwest, east to the Atlantic Coast, and north to southern Canada. There were many different tribes with various customs, but their basic way of life depended on using the resources of the forest.

One Woodland tribe was the Menominee, who live in Wisconsin, mostly in an area bounded by Lake Superior and Lake Michigan. Green Bay, off Lake Michigan, was their main base. A river that empties into the bay bears their name. Their homeland, covered with coniferous (cone-bearing) and mixed hardwood trees, was at the fringe of the Woodlands region. To the west lay the prairies and plains, with wide-open spaces where buffalo thrived. The Menominee relied upon the forest, but they also ventured west onto the prairies to hunt buffalo, as did the Plains Indians. Like most Native Americans who lived east of the Rockies in southern Canada or the northern United States, the Menominee spoke a dialect, or variation, of the Algonquin language. Algonquin speakers who lived near one another had little problem communicating because they spoke similar dialects. Groups that lived far apart, however, found it more difficult to understand one another. The language spoken by the Menominee was somewhat unusual because it was considerably different from the dialects of most speakers of the Algonquin language.

Origins of the Menominee

During the Ice Ages, much of the area that became the home of Woodland people was covered by glaciers. This region was not habitable. South of the

glaciers were vast plains, windswept and cold for most of the year. Great herds of big-game animals, such as mammoths and giant bison, roamed these grasslands. These herds provided a bonanza of food for Native Americans who lived on the plains. Over time, they devised cooperative hunting methods to provide a steady supply of food.

About 12,000 years ago, the Ice Ages ended. The glaciers began to melt and slowly shrank to the north. The air began to warm. Trees began to grow on the plains east of the Mississippi River. Ice Age game animals disappeared, partly because of climatic change but also because so many of them had been killed by humans.

Small groups of Native Americans moved into the region once occupied by glaciers. The people lived by hunting woodland animals—deer, for example—and gathering wild plants. Wild rice was a key food for the Menominee. In fact, their name means "rice people." The Menominee also ate fish and shellfish from the freshwaters of lakes and streams. Between 2,000 and 3,000 years ago, agriculture spread into the Woodlands from the south. The chief crop was corn, developed from a wild plant that grows in Mexico and Central America. Other crops were pumpkins and beans. Some tribes called corn, squash, and beans the "three sisters." The northern forests of the Woodlands were not as suitable for farming as lands farther south. So even though Woodland tribes raised crops, they also depended on wild animals and plants.

Scholars do not know much about the lifestyle of the Menominee before their first contact with Europeans late in the seventeenth century. One reason for this is that European influence quickly changed the Menominee's way of life. The Menominee's first recorded contact with Europeans was an exchange with a French fur trader named Nicolas Perrot in 1667. It is believed that some European goods began to reach the Menominee from other Native Americans even before that date.

Originally, the entire Menominee tribe lived near the mouth of the Menominee River on Green Bay. Then disaster struck. From New York, the powerful Iroquois, armed with guns provided by Dutch traders, began to advance westward. Although they did not initially threaten the Menominee, they pushed several other tribes of Algonquin-speaking people into Menominee country. Eventually, the Menominee, the neighboring Winnebago, and the Algonquin-speaking refugees learned to get along and support one another. After years of warfare, they drove the Iroquois from their lands for good. The Menominee who survived ended up living in a single village, where the Europeans first encountered them. Records indicate that the entire tribe numbered only a few hundred people, including forty warriors. As years passed, however, the Menominee's numbers increased, and they again became a strong fighting force among Native American tribes.

Daily Life

The Menominee built two different types of housing, one for summer, the other for winter. During the summer, they lived in rectangular, peaked cabins made of bark slabs held together by trimmed saplings. Their winter homes were dome-shaped lodges, sometimes called *wigwams*. A *wigwam* was made by bending saplings in a U-shape and then covering them with bark or mats of reeds. Like other Native Americans of the Woodlands region, the Menominee may have slept on raised platforms of wood that were covered with mats and placed near the walls of the house.

Since the Menominee depended largely on wild rice and fish for food, they were expert at canoeing. They made two types of canoes. One was of birch bark covering a frame of wood. The other was a dugout, crafted from a hollowed-out log.

Menominee tools and weapons included bows and arrows, and war clubs for hunting and fighting, as well as knives of copper, stone, and shell. They also had stone axes for building their homes. The shells of freshwater clams and snails were widely used by the Menominee for utensils, and even as dishes. The Menominee made baskets and bags of woven plant fiber, buffalo hair, animal skins, and bark. Bowls were made from gourds (vegetables with thick rinds) that were hollowed out with large stones. Buckets were

Opposite: The dome-shaped wigwam was built to withstand winter weather.

Snowshoes, such as the one this man is making, enabled the Menominee to walk in the winter Woodlands without sinking in the snow.

made of birch bark, and pottery was crafted from clay. Plant fibers and the tendons of animals provided rope and string.

Like other Native Americans, the Menominee decorated many of their implements. They placed geometric designs on their pottery. On medicine bags—pouches used to hold sacred objects—they used animal hair and porcupine quills to create the images of spirits from their religion.

Family Life

According to early reports, before European contact some Menominee men had more than one wife.

Marriages were arranged between families, although possibly only after a couple had expressed an interest in one another. The families of the future husband and wife exchanged presents before the marriage. Once married, a woman moved into her husband's household, which he headed.

As in many European cultures, the Menominee family was an extended one. Uncles, aunts, cousins, and grandparents all had key roles in family functions. Once a marriage occurred, relatives on both sides became very influential in family affairs. Nephews and uncles, for example, were closely bound in times of war. Neither was allowed to desert the other on the battlefield. Each was bound to avenge the other's death.

Menominee men generally carried on the hunting and fishing. The men also were in charge of religious ceremonies and made the objects used in these rites. It was a man's job to make weapons, tools, canoes, nets, and traps. Women raised crops, gathered wild plant foods and firewood, carried water to camp, and took household items along when traveling. Menominee women made clothes and household utensils. They dressed the animal skins and wove mats and baskets. It is believed, however, that occasionally men and women shared one another's work. Women sometimes hunted and fished with the men. Men, in turn, may have helped women with the gathering of wild plants.

Rearing children was a well-organized and important activity for the Menominee. Very young children were kept close to their mothers. Until they could walk, they were often strapped onto wooden cradle boards, which

Children are taught at an early age to respect and care for animals.

were worn by their mothers like backpacks. That way a mother could keep her baby with her while her hands were free to work. Mothers nursed their children for as long as their babies wanted milk. Gradually, the children learned to accept other types of food, but the process took time.

As a child grew older, he or she gathered with other youngsters to listen to the elder people of the tribe talk of Menominee traditions and values. Elders would instruct children on the correct way to live and, especially, the value of self-control. Older adults observed the children to see if they acted in an unusual or unhappy fashion, then tried to help them out of potential trouble. Some Menominee elders were experts in "baby talk," and they could communicate with the very young.

As future warriors and hunters, boys received special attention. They underwent tough physical training. The region in which the Menominee lived had very severe winters. Boys of only seven or eight years of age were taught to endure cold temperatures by breaking through ice in a lake or stream and bathing in the chilly water. Then they rolled in the snow.

A Menominee boy has a quiet moment with his horse. Good horsemanship is traditionally a valued skill.

This mother is always within reach of her child, who is strapped to a cradle board.

Men built birch-bark canoes for navigating the rivers and lakes of the Woodlands.

Menominee women tended and harvested the wild rice.

Food

Although the Menominee had vegetable gardens, they lived mostly on plants and animals found in the forests, lakes, and streams. Wild rice, which grows in shallow water, was perhaps the most important food. The

Menominee cared for wild rice as if they had planted it themselves. They tended the rice and guarded it from animals. Women made twine out of fibers from the basswood tree and tied the rice heads together to keep birds from taking them. In the fall, when the rice was ripe, the Menominee harvested

A man boils the sap collected from maple trees in order to make maple syrup.

it while kneeling in canoes. They removed the husks by shaking the grains in skin bags. Then the rice was dried and stored for use during the rest of the year.

During the early spring, the Menominee tapped maple trees for sap and boiled it into syrup. Entire families would make temporary camps in areas of the forest where sugar maples—called *michtan* by the Menominee—were abundant. Sap flowed when the bark of a maple was cut, and the sap was collected in buckets. When the sap was boiled, most of the water it contained evaporated, leaving behind a thick, sugary syrup. By late summer, the Menominee began to collect wild forest plants, such as berries and ferns, as well as mushrooms and other fungi. As nuts ripened in the fall, these, too, were collected by the tribe and stored in baskets for the winter. Wild game was another key food source, and fish such as bass, suckers, and especially sturgeon, were even more important.

Hunting and Fishing

Like other Woodland peoples, the Menominee were skilled at stalking game in the forest. The Woodlands were like a vast butcher shop—only instead of paying for their food with money, they hunted it. Probably the most important game animal was the white-tailed deer. Deer meat was low in fat and very healthy. It was easily smoked in strips over a fire. Dried deer meat could be stored for many months. It could be eaten plain or added to soups and stews. Because it was light-weight and very nutritious, dried meat was ideal for carrying on long trips,

such as hunting excursions or migrations between summer and winter encampments. Deer tendons could be made into bow strings, hides into clothing, and bones and antlers into many different types of implements.

A host of other animals were available to the Menominee, including wild turkeys, geese and ducks, black bears, raccoons, and small rodents.

Small animals were caught with traps or snares. Lone hunters, armed with bow and arrow, could stalk or ambush larger creatures, such as deer. Often, however, the Menominee hunted in groups, using cooperative hunting tactics to drive and surround large game animals.

The Menominee occasionally hunted buffalo. Small numbers of them roamed Menominee country, and at the edges of the prairies, to the west, large populations of these huge animals could be found. One buffalo provided a large quantity of food. While a big deer might furnish 150 pounds of meat, a buffalo could weigh more than 1,000 pounds.

Since fish were so important to the Menominee for food, the men spent considerable time trying to catch them. Fish were netted or trapped in devices made of sticks. They were also speared from the banks of streams or from canoes, traditionally at night. A painting done by an artist in 1845, when many of the Menominee still lived by the old ways, shows this method. Menominee fishermen set out in birch-bark canoes, two men to a vessel. One of them, in the stern, or back, paddled. The other stood near the bow, the front, with his fish spear at the ready. Mounted on a wooden pole at the bow

Fishing was often done at night. Torches were lit
and placed in front of the canoe to attract fish
and make them easier to spear.

was a blazing torch. Its firelight attracted fish toward the surface of the water and made them easy for the spear man to see. Fishing did not stop during the winter. The Menominee cut holes in the ice covering lakes and streams, and then netted or speared the fish through the holes.

Political and Social Organization

Ancient Menominee tradition tells how the people descended from two spiritual beings—the Bear and Eagle, also called the Thunderbird. According to Menominee legend, the Bear made himself into a human form and called upon the Eagle to do the same. Each gathered about himself other animal

The elders in the Menominee community are still respected for their knowledge of tradition.

spirits, such as the Beaver and Sturgeon, which also assumed human shapes. Eventually, tribal legends say, the Bear and Eagle families decided to live together in a village, and they became the Menominee tribe. Part of the tribe owed allegiance to the Bear, and the remainder to the Eagle. Within each group were clans that traced themselves back to the other animal beings that had followed the Bear and the Eagle. Clan membership was handed down through the male side of the family.

It is suspected that before European contact, the members of the tribe who governed civil affairs were drawn from the Bear group. The hereditary chief of the Bear group served as the tribe's head, although he had limited authority. The Eagle group supplied the tribe's war leaders. The elders of each of the clans made up a tribal council, which was chaired by the Bear group chief. The council seems to have advised and made certain decisions about tribal life. It is doubtful, however, that the council was a law-making body. From childhood, each member of the tribe was taught a code of behavior designed to make tribal society work smoothly. The Menominee learned self-restraint, for example, and responsibility toward others.

Perhaps the most organized unit of Menominee society was the war party, led by a notable warrior. Most conflicts did not involve the entire tribe. Usually, small groups of warriors set out on raids against enemy tribes, often to dispute the enemy's rights to Menominee hunting territories.

Opposite: According to Menominee legend, the Bear gave himself a human shape and became one of the people's spiritual ancestors.

Clothing

Early European explorers reported that the Menominee wore few clothes. The most common garments, for women as well as men, were breechcloths and leggings, usually made of deerskin.

Leggings were worn as much for protection against heavy brush and brambles as for warmth.

During the summer, the Menominee usually went barefoot, but in the winter they wore deerskin moccasins. When it was particularly cold, they wrapped the upper parts of their bodies in furs taken from animals they trapped. Soon after they came into contact with Europeans, however, the Menominee replaced their fur wraps with blankets, which they got from

The man is dressed in deerskin clothing. The woman is wearing a dress made out of European cloth. On her lap, she wears a blanket for warmth.

22

traders. Once they saw the dresses worn by European women, Menominee women quickly adapted to wearing them.

Both men and women of the tribe allowed their hair to grow long. The men often wore roaches, or crests, made of deer fur and eagle feathers. Fur headdresses (elaborate coverings for the head) were also worn by some of the men. Finely tanned capes of deerskin werc worn on special occasions, such as ceremonies. The Menominee attending a ceremony rubbed grease and oil into his hair and on his body, which was also painted with sacred designs.

Games

The Menominee played games for fun, but their play had another purpose as well. Games were sacred. They were played, for example, to honor spirits or cure disease. Two Native American games are still played today—lacrosse and an early version of ice hockey. Lacrosse—named by the French—was especially important. It is a rough sport today, but it was even tougher when early Native American men engaged in it. They wore no uniforms or pads— usually only breechcloths.

The object of lacrosse was similar then to what it is today. Each of two teams defended a goal at either end of a playing field. Each team member carried a lacrosse stick, which was curved at the end. A small, woven net was attached to the curved portion of the stick. With this net, players caught and threw a ball made of wood or animal hide, trying to hurl it across the opposing team's goal line.

A brightly colored headdress is worn by a young Menominee man.

Women competed in a similar game called *shinny*, which was an early form of hockey that was played with a ball and sticks similar to those used in lacrosse. Variations of this game were popular among many Native American tribes. Today's hockey fans owe a great debt to the Native Americans who first developed the game. Gambling with dice thrown into a bowl was another pastime of the Menominee. So were foot races, in which both men and women participated.

Religious Life

Roman Catholic priests of the Jesuit order were among the first Europeans to visit the Menominee. They learned that the Menominee religion recognized many different spirits. The Menominee, like the followers of Christianity, believed that there was an eternal tug-of-war between spirits representing goodness—who live above the Earth—and evil spirits below. The Earth, according to ancient Menominee religious tradition, was an island, floating in an endless ocean between the two groups of spirits. They were found on eight levels—four above the Earth, four below. As distance from the Earth increased, so did the strength of the spirits' powers. The evil spirit farthest from Earth was represented by the

Great White Bear. Highest above the Earth was the Supreme Being who dominated all others. The Earth itself was believed to be inhabited by other spirits. Some were good, such as the elf that helped people sleep by tapping them on the head with a soft club. Others were evil, such as the skeleton who haunted the forests and the cannibalistic giants who preyed on people.

The Menominee also believed that every species of animal had its own special spirit who watched over it. Although they killed animals because they needed meat to survive, the people had a special reverence for wildlife and the spirits that were assigned to each type of creature.

It was important for every Menominee to gain contact with the spirit

A Dream Dance drum

Menominee dancers perform the Dream Dance
in order to get in touch with the spirit world.

world in order to tap into its power. To do this, they often sought the help of medicine men, or shamans. These were people who had demonstrated a special ability to reach the spirit world. For example, they knew how to interpret dreams. They also were gifted in the use of plants to fight disease and cure wounds. Each Menominee sought the help of his or her own guardian spirit, who would provide strength and guidance for a lifetime. The spirit was found through a ceremony that many Native Americans call a "vision quest." It was literally a search for a dream that, once interpreted by a shaman, would set a person's course for the rest of his or her life. The quest began at a very young age. Young boys and girls were required to fast for short periods—a day, perhaps two. Children were taught to open their minds to the spiritual realm. Their training was difficult. What lay ahead was even more demanding.

The end of the quest took place at puberty. With face painted black, a young Menominee entered a small *wigwam*, where he or she hoped to commune with the guardian spirit. The *wigwam* held no food or water. The young person entering the *wigwam* was called *mesahkatewew*—he or she who fasts. For about ten days, the young person neither ate nor drank. If all went well, a dream was experienced. Usually, the key figure in the dream was an animal. When the dream was over, a shaman consulted the young man or woman. The shaman described the powers that had been given to the dreamer—and also rules the dreamer had to follow to benefit from them. Most people followed these rules carefully until they died.

Jesuit priests from Canada were some of the first white people to establish relations with the Menominee.

European Contact

The Woodland tribes living along the Atlantic Coast of North America encountered Europeans suddenly. The coastal tribes were living traditional lifestyles when they first met people from beyond the ocean. Tribes further west, such as the Menominee, were

affected by European influences long before they ever met one of the newcomers to the North American continent. Native Americans had far-flung trading routes. In the early 1600s, items traded by Europeans for goods from the coastal Indians quickly reached the tribes of the western Woodlands. Even before the French fur trader Nicolas Perrot met them, the Menominee were probably using some European trade goods, such as metal knives.

Toward the end of the seventeenth century, French explorers and Jesuit priests from Canada began to establish direct contacts with the Menominee. By the beginning of the eighteenth century, French fur traders were regularly doing business with the Menominee, who had become one of the most powerful tribes in the Western Great Lakes region.

The Menominee's social structure changed: The tribe divided into nine bands, probably according to clans. Each band had its own summer village. In the winter, the bands fanned out over the countryside, trapping beaver and other fur-bearing animals. They traded the skins with the French in exchange for firearms. The arms and the overall support of the French helped the Menominee to become a powerful tribe again. In return, the Menominee supplied the French with furs. They also provided warriors to fight the British when the two European powers clashed over the right to establish colonies in North America.

In 1761, after the British had beaten the French, they established relations with the Menominee. When, in 1763,

Chief Pontiac of the Ottawa tribe led an uprising of several tribes against the British, the Menominee fought on the British side. Even after the American Revolution, the British continued to exert a powerful influence on the Menominee. In 1794, a treaty between Britain and the United States recognized that the region including Menominee country was a U.S. territory. Even so, the Menominee remained close to the British in nearby Canada. During the War of 1812, Menominee warriors fought with their British allies against the Americans. Not until 1815, when the Americans established a Native American agency and trading post at Green Bay, did the tribe come under the control of the United States. The Menominee gradually transferred their allegiance to the Americans. A band of fifty Menominee warriors helped U.S. forces defeat Chief Blackhawk, who led a desperate bid by the Sauk and Fox tribes to resist American settlement.

During the early years of American rule, the Menominee experienced a period of difficult change. In 1818, the territory inhabited by the tribe became part of the Michigan Territory. Within a few years, white settlers began moving into the area. Then, in 1836, the new territory of Wisconsin was formed. It encompassed the Menominee tribal area. Within fifteen years there were 300,000 whites in Wisconsin.

During this period of time, Menominee lands were taken from the tribe in huge chunks. In 1831, while the lands were still part of the Michigan Territory, the tribe received about five cents per acre for a half-million acres. The property was given to members of eastern Woodland tribes who had been displaced from their homes. In the same year, the Menominee signed a treaty giving the U.S. government two-and-a-half-million acres, again for about a nickel an acre. Additional treaties in 1836 and 1848 cost the tribe even more land. Four years later, in 1852, most of the tribe settled on the reservation that they occupy today. It was placed under the jurisdiction of the federal government in 1854.

The Menominee Today

The Menominee reservation, with headquarters in the community of Keshena, was northwest of Green Bay. Once the Menominee moved onto the reservation, they spread out through its forest wilderness. Most of them tried to continue to live as they had in the past. As time passed, however, they began to adapt to ways of white people. They started logging for commercial purposes in 1872, and by the 1880s, lumbering was an important source of money for the tribe. In 1888, the U.S. government attempted to stop the Menominee's growing timber industry. The U.S. attorney general ruled that the tribe had the right to live on the reservation, but they could not sell timber cut there. Congress passed an act that allowed the tribe's timber industry to continue, however. In 1906, a railway depot was established on the reservation, and then in 1923, the state highways reached the Menominee. Postal and telephone services arrived as well.

In 1953, the federal government started a new policy toward Native American people. Until then, tribal reservations were largely free of state laws and regulations and received financial assistance and support from the federal government. Vast numbers of Native Americans needed this assistance to survive. Under the new policy, state governments would have authority over Native Americans. The policy was first applied to the Menominee in

A Menominee medicine lodge

A Menominee woman poses with her partially completed basket.

1954, when jurisdiction over the reservation fell to the state of Wisconsin. Without federal aid, and subject to Wisconsin law, the Menominee suffered. Their economy was in shambles. In 1971, President Richard Nixon declared that placing Native Americans under state authority was a bad policy. A law was passed ending the policy, and the Menominee reservation again came under the wing of the federal government. In 1977, a constitution was created establishing a tribal government.

The present Menominee reservation covers 235,033 acres. According to information supplied by the Wisconsin Bureau of Indian Affairs, as of 1993, there are 3,692 people on the Menominee reservation. According to the 1990 U.S. census, the Menominee number 7,543 nationwide.

Today, the Menominee have a nine-member tribal legislature, headed by a chairperson. Members are elected in January at three-year intervals. The tribe has its own court system and police department. Sources of revenue for the tribe include a supermarket and two gambling businesses where the Menominee offer bingo and a casino. Another agency of the tribe oversees other business ventures, largely lumbering and a sawmill. Although most members of the Menominee tribe now have a lifestyle similar to that of other Americans, many of them are committed to preserving the ancient traditions of their people in a modern world.

Chronology

1667   The French fur trader Nicolas Perrot exchanges goods with the Menominee.

1761   Following the French and Indian War, British influence replaces that of the French.

1763   Menominee warriors help the British fight the forces of Chief Pontiac.

1815   The United States establishes an agency for Native Americans and a trading post at Green Bay.

1818   Menominee country is included in the Michigan Territory.

1831   The Menominee tribe sells a half-million acres, and then two-and-a-half-million acres, to the U.S. government at about five cents an acre.

1836   Menominee country is included in the new Wisconsin Territory.

1852   The tribe moves to a federal reservation.

1872   The Menominee start a timber industry.

1906   Railroad track and a depot come to the reservation.

1923   The reservation is linked to the state highway system.

1954   The federal government, under a new policy, terminates its authority over the reservation.

1971   President Richard Nixon declares that termination policy is a mistake and reinstates federal authority.

1977   A new Menominee tribal constitution is approved.

INDEX

Acknowledgments and Photo Credits

Cover and all artwork by Richard Smolinski.
Photographs on pages 9, 10, 20, and 23: ©Steven L. Raymer/National Geographic Image Collection; pages 24, 29, and 30: ©State Historical Society of Wisconsin (WHi(x3)18851; WHi(x3)32756; WHi(x3)26184).
Map by Blackbirch Graphics, Inc.